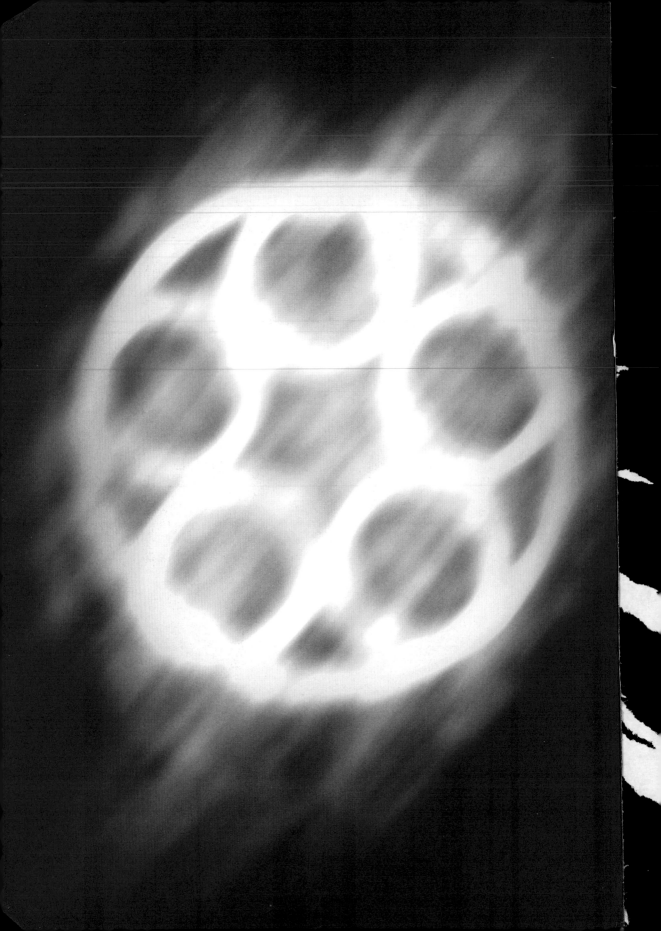

ANTHONY HOROWITZ

THE POWER OF FIVE: BOOK ONE

RAVEN'S GATE

THE GRAPHIC NOVEL

adapted by TONY LEE

illustrated by
DOM REARDON &
LEE O'CONNOR

WALKER

First published 2010 by Walker Books Ltd
87 Vauxhall Walk, London SE11 5HJ

This edition published 2013

10 9 8 7 6 5 4 3 2 1

Text and illustrations © 2010 Walker Books Ltd

Based on the original novel *Raven's Gate*
© 1983, 2005 Stormbreaker Productions Limited

Power of 5 logo™ © 2010 Walker Books Limited

Anthony Horowitz has asserted his moral rights.

This book has been typeset in CC Dave Gibbons

Printed and bound in Singapore

British Library Cataloguing in Publication Data:
a catalogue record for this book is available from the
British Library

ISBN 978-1-4063-4498-1

www.walker.co.uk

www.powerof5.co.uk

Before the beginning ∴
was the gate ∴   ∴   ∴
And five gatekeepers ∴   ∴

                       children

Four boys. One girl.

          it has been written

          The night of everlasting
darkness is drawing in.

The gate is about to open.
   The gatekeepers must return.

"SO, WHERE IS HE?"

"HER NAME IS *JAYNE DEVERILL* –"

"– AND SHE SHOULD BE HERE ANY MINUTE NOW."

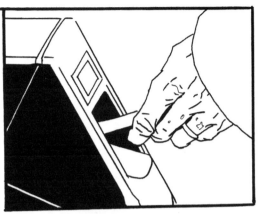

"NOWHERE!"

baltimoreravens...
400 x 300 - 1...
thischicksviewonespor...

Raven
x 360 - 17k - jpg
kaweahoaks.com

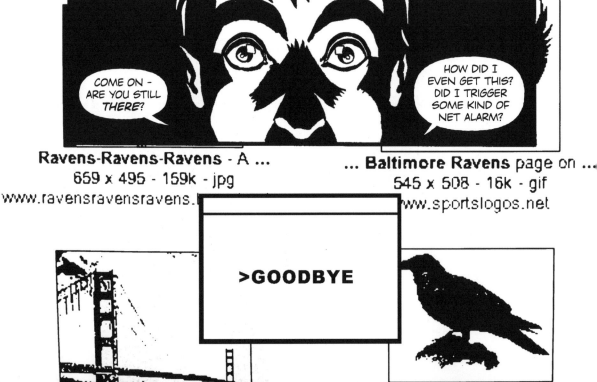

Ravens-Ravens-Ravens - A ...
659 x 495 - 159k - jpg
www.ravensravensravens. ...

... Baltimore Ravens page on ...
545 x 508 - 16k - gif
www.sportslogos.net

"MATTHEW, WAKE UP."

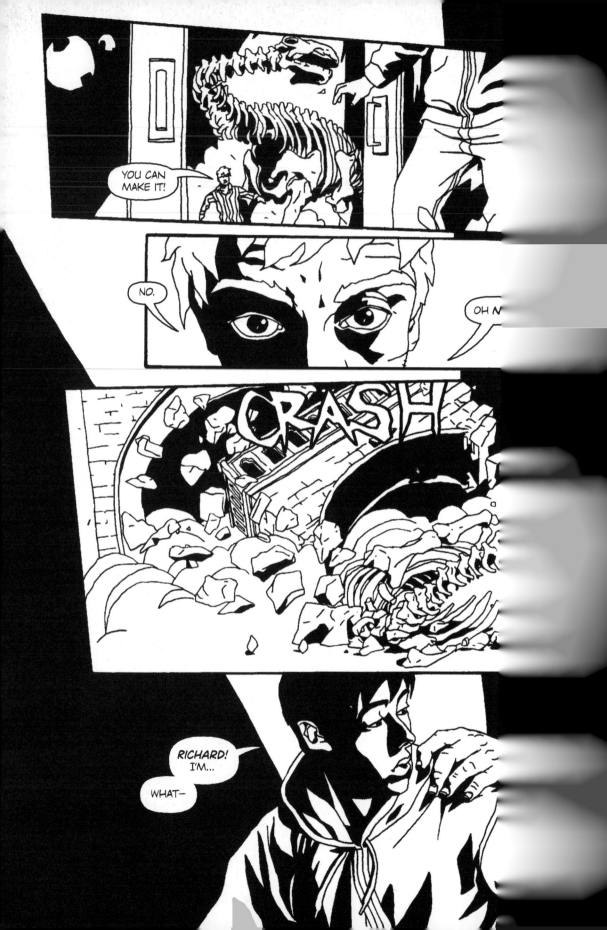

END OF BOOK ONE

ANTHONY HOROWITZ is the author of the number one bestselling Alex Rider books and The Power of Five series. He has enjoyed huge success as a writer for both children and adults, most recently with his highly acclaimed Sherlock Holmes novel, *The House of Silk*.

He has won numerous awards, including the Bookseller/Nielsen Author of the Year Award, The Children's Book of the Year Award at the British Book Awards, and the Red House Children's Book Award.
Anthony has also created and written many major television series, including *Injustice*, *Collision* and the award-winning *Foyle's War*.

You can find out more about Anthony and his books at:
www.anthonyhorowitz.com
www.alexrider.com
www.powerof5.co.uk

TONY LEE, has been a writer for over twenty years. He started his career mainly in games journalism, but in the early nineties moved into writing for radio, TV and magazines.

In 2004 Tony turned his attention to comics writing and has since worked for a variety of publishers, including Marvel Comics, IDW Publishing, Markosia, Rebellion, Panini and Titan. He has contributed to many popular and high-profile properties such as *X-Men*, *Spider Man*, *Starship Troopers*, *Wallace & Gromit* and *Shrek*. He is currently the writer of the ongoing Doctor Who comic series for IDW Publishing.

In 2010 Tony became a New York Times #1 Best Selling Graphic Novelist for his adaptation of *Pride & Prejudice & Zombies*: *The Graphic Novel*. He is the author of *Outlaw*: *The Legend of Robin Hood* and *Excalibur*: *The Legend of King Arthur* also published by Walker Books. Tony lives in London.

www.tonylee.co.uk

DOM REARDON is a British comics artist, whose work appears mainly in the British comic 2000*AD*. Lee O'Connor is an illustrator whose work has appeared in the cult European comics magazine HEAVY METAL, the popular PHONOGRAM series from Image Comics, the IRAQ graphic novel published by the international humanitarian charity War on Want and numerous anthologies, small press and indie comics on both sides of the Atlantic.

LEE O'CONNOR'S illustrations have appeared in magazines and on book covers, and he has storyboarded for film and music video. His artwork has been exhibited in London, he's lectured on Illustration in Australia and painted murals in New Zealand. Lee lives in the wilds of rural Devon, next to an Iron Age hill fort.

www.leeoconnor.com

Collect all the Alex Rider books:

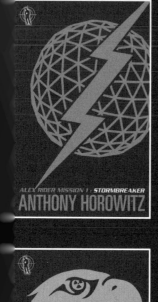

ALEX RIDER MISSION 1 : STORMBREAKER
ANTHONY HOROWITZ

ALEX RIDER MISSION 2 : POINT BLANC
ANTHONY HOROWITZ

ALEX RIDER MISSION 3 : SKELETON KEY
ANTHONY HOROWITZ

ALEX RIDER MISSION 4 : EAGLE STRIKE
ANTHONY HOROWITZ

ALEX RIDER MISSION 5 : SCORPIA
ANTHONY HOROWITZ

ALEX RIDER MISSION 6 : ARK ANGEL
ANTHONY HOROWITZ

ALEX RIDER MISSION 7 : SNAKEHEAD
ANTHONY HOROWITZ

ALEX RIDER MISSION 8 : CROCODILE TEARS
ANTHONY HOROWITZ

ALEX RIDER MISSION 9 : SCORPIA RISING
ANTHONY HOROWITZ